Kindness
for
Koalas

Designed by Tabitha Blore
Edited by Lesley Sims
Design Manager: Nicola Butler

Usborne House, 83-85 Saffron Hill,
London EC1N 8RT, England

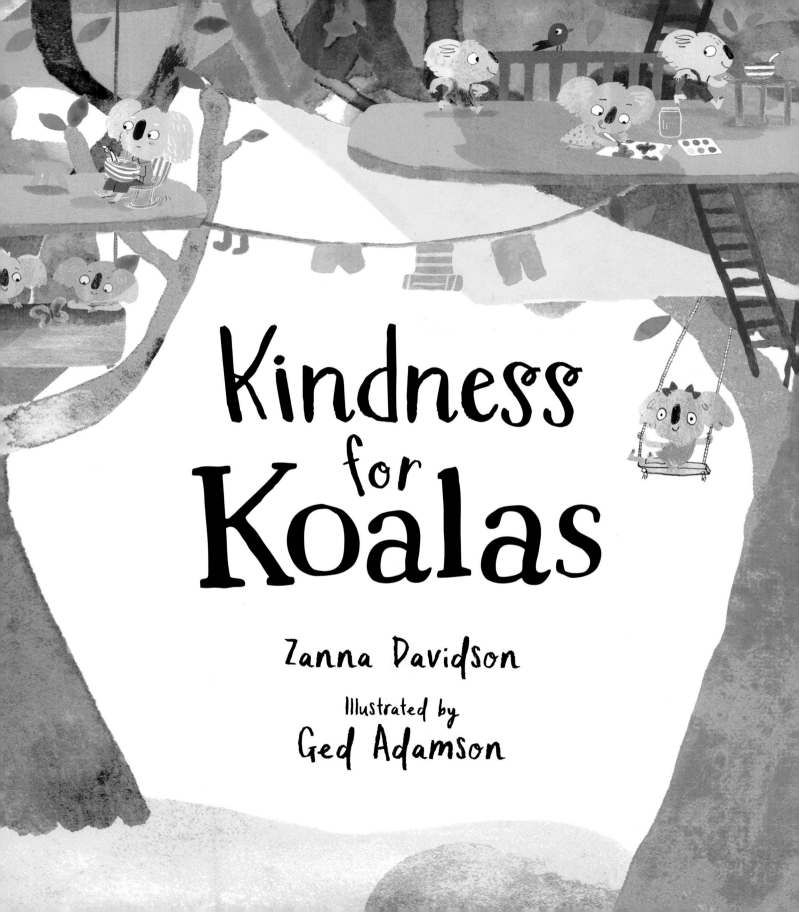

Kindness
for
Koalas

Zanna Davidson

Illustrated by
Ged Adamson

Meet Mala the koala. She's having a bad day.

She slipped

and **tripped**

and **stumbled**...

Why does NOTHING go my way?

"My bowl's been smashed to pieces.
There's **breakfast** on my dress!
And the picture that I painted
is a **scrumpled**, **soggy** mess."

"Now everything is ruined. I'm feeling really CRUMMY!
There's a prickle in my eyes and a soreness in my TUMMY."

She **stomped** into the forest,
crossly **pulling** at the leaves.

She **trampled** on the flowers

and was **beastly** to the bees.

She **shouted** at the birds
in a mean and humphy grump...

...then **slumped** down with a **sigh**
on a little wooden stump.

But then she heard a **rustling**. A mouse stood by her side.
"I think that I can guess," she said, "just how you feel **inside**."

"You've gone all tight and knotty.
You're full of angry thoughts.
You think **EVERYONE'S** to blame,
and **EVERYTHING'S** at fault.

But there's a simple answer.
I promise you will find,
you'll soon start feeling better
if **you** do something **KIND**."

Mala stopped her sniffling. And then she wiped her eyes.

"Okay, Miss Mouse," she whispered. "I suppose it's worth a *try*."

Mala started walking,
beside a sparkling stream.
"But **HOW** can I be kind?"

What does kindness
really mean?

Her thoughts were interrupted by a troop of kangaroos.

They came **bouncing** though the forest,

and **bounded** into view.

Mala called and waved, but they wouldn't slow their pace.
"Can't stop! Can't talk! Can't listen!
We're trying to win a race!"

But a spiky little creature,
who was waddling behind,
said, **"I'll help you if I can..."**

Can you teach me
to be KIND?

The creature smiled and scratched his head.
"Well now, let me see.
I suppose I need to ponder...
what does **kindness** mean to me?"

"It's being there when needed. It's putting others first,

and being your **best** self, even when you're at your worst.

It's not just for koalas, or even kangaroos…
Remember that **all** creatures deserve your kindness too."

Mala waved and thanked him as he waddled on his way,
but still she felt **unsure**…

How can I be
kind today?

Just then she heard a weeping –
a lonely, sorry sound.
It was coming from a baby bat,
huddled on the ground.

"I fell out of my tree,"
she squeaked.

And now I can't get **back!**

And Mala smiled. "Aha!" she said.

Now *I* can help with that!

Mala felt a little lighter, as she carried on her way,
as if by being kind herself, she'd brightened up her day.

I've done an act of kindness.
I'll stop and have a treat!

But before she started eating,
she heard a peep!

peep!

peep!

Ten fluffy emu chicks came by, and Papa Emu too.

"Can I ask…?" said Mala.

What does kindness mean to you?

"I think," said Papa Emu,
"it's showing that you care.
With a friendly smile or hug,
or by offering to share."

Mala's eyes grew round. "This is my **greatest** test.
Kindness isn't always easy… but I will do my **best**."

She reached into her pocket,
"I don't have much to spare,
but would you like to try my treats?"

I **think**
I'd like to share.

A warm glow filled her tummy, from being kind again.
She felt as if, by sharing, she had made eleven friends!
And as Mala wandered on, she thought of what she'd done.

"I've **helped**,

I've **shared**,

I've **listened!**

I wonder what's to come..."

When she turned the corner,
there, sitting on a stone,
was her friend, the little wombat,
looking **sad** and all **alone**.

"Do you want to talk?" she asked. "You look so very blue...
I'm here to try and help you. Just tell me what to do."

Wombat gave a teary smile, and then he dried his eyes.

Would you mind just sitting here,
and being by my side?

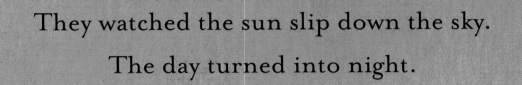

They watched the sun slip down the sky.
The day turned into night.

Your kindness is
like starlight.
It shines so clear
and bright.

Wombat smiled at Mala.
"You're the very **best** of friends."

I've one more thing
to do now.
It's time to make
amends.

She said sorry to
the flowers she'd hurt,
and sorry to the bees.

She left presents for the birds,
in the branches of their trees.

"And now it's time for bed.
I feel warm and good inside."
But then she heard a rustling,
and the mouse stood by her side.

Oh Mala, can you tell me
all the things you learned today?
Did you discover kindness
in all its wondrous ways?

"Now let me see..." said Mala,
and she stood and thought a while.
"I've found out something magical!"
she answered with a smile.

Kindness is the little things –
not showy, big or grand.
It's comforting a friend,
or holding someone's hand.

"You've learned so much," the mouse replied. "There's one more thing to do…"

You've been kind **all day** to others – now make sure you're kind to **you!**

Mala yawned and rubbed her eyes.
"I think I need a rest,
and something else as well besides,
that koalas can do **best**!

It makes me feel so happy –
safe and warm and snug.
I'll end my busy day with..."

"A BIG KOALA HUG!"

z z z